For Oliver and Harry—my own very special superheroes.
For Nicholas, who helped me to be brave enough to write my stories.
And for all the little superheroes who face their own fears every single day. —K. T.

For every mom out there—you are the biggest superheroes I know. —C. E.

SUPERHEROES DON'T GET SCARED

...OR DO THEY?

By Kate Thompson

Art by Clare Elsom

VIKING

Maisie Brown was
feeling scared
and oh-so-very small.

"It's just not fair,"
she cried out loud.
"I don't feel brave at all!"

"I **wish** I were a superhero flying through the air.
I'd battle all the baddies in my bright red underwear!"

But Maisie frowned and shook her head.
"That *can't* be true at all!
Burpnado flies around to look
for trouble, big and small."

"From jiggly-wiggly jellyfish
to **wobbly jelly** treats,
they make her want to run away
and **hide** beneath her sheets."

"I bet Specstacular," said Maisie,
"never feels afraid.
When anyone's in danger,
she comes dashing to their aid!"

"She spots the baddies from afar
and sets her specs to MAX.
Then, ZAP! Out shoots a Super Ray,
which stops them in their tracks!"

ZAP!

"In fact,"

said Mom,

"there is one thing
that takes away her spark.
Specstacular is terrified
of being in the…"

"...DARK!"

"She panics when she cannot see.
It makes her want to sob.
She always takes Night-Vision Specs
to each and every job."

"All right," said Maisie with a frown,
"but BoogieBoy's bravetastic!
His boogie-blasts are sticky, strong,
and ever so elastic!"

"From slimy slugs to wiggly worms
and even *teeny* ants,
they scare poor BoogieBoy so much,
he **jumps** out of his pants!"

"Okay," said Maisie slowly,
"but when Jelly Blob attacked,
Burpnado burped him up to space!
I know that for a FACT!"

"And after Blackout Burglar Bat
switched off the moon and sun,
Specstacular raced through the dark,
not stopping till she won!"

"And just last week, when Disco Bug
forced everyone to dance,
brave BoogieBoy launched boogie balls
that stopped the bugs mid-prance!"

Maisie smiled and crossed her arms.
"You see, you are quite wrong.
No superhero's *ever* scared.
They are too brave and strong."

Dad shuffled close to Maisie and then whispered in her ear, "But bravery cannot exist unless you first feel...

"To feel afraid is normal, and it happens to us all.
Your tummy flutters, flips, and flops.
It makes you feel so small.
But when you choose to face your fear,
whatever it may be,
then something magic happens…"

"You may not battle baddies or bring crime down to zero,
but you would still be just as brave as any superhero."

Maisie smiled. She still felt scared, but that was now okay.

"Just call me SUPER MAISIE! I am feeling brave today!"

VIKING

An imprint of Penguin Random House LLC, New York

First published in the United States of America by Viking,
an imprint of Penguin Random House LLC, 2022
First published in Great Britain in 2020 by Upside Down Books, an imprint of
Trigger Publishing

Visit us online at penguinrandomhouse.com.

Library of Congress Cataloging-in-Publication Data is available.

Manufactured in China

ISBN 9780593352618

TOPL

1 3 5 7 9 10 8 6 4 2

Edited by Liza Kaplan · Designed by Marcia Wong · Text set in Grad

Helping children understand their emotions as well as identifying the same feelings in other people is an important step in their emotional well-being and positive mental health. *Superheroes Don't Get Scared is* a brilliant and insightful book, which normalizes the experience of fear and anxiety, as well as encouraging children to face their fears and find their inner (super)powers.

It's a very humorous book, and children will love the fun characters and their exciting adventures. Perhaps most importantly, they will also be able to relate to Maisie and the message at its heart: that fear is felt by even the bravest hero . . . and that's okay, because to recognize fear is the first step in facing it. Everyone will enjoy reading this story—parents, children, and superheroes alike!

Lauren Callaghan

consultant clinical psychologist,
co-founder and clinical director of Trigger Publishing